Excuse M

MANNERS ALWAYS MATTER

Illustrated by Lance Raichert
Written by Caleb Burroughs

Copyright © 2005 Publications International, Ltd. All rights reserved.
This publication may not be reproduced in whole or in part by
any means whatsoever without written permission from
Louis Weber, C.E.O., Publications International, Ltd.
7373 North Cicero Avenue, Lincolnwood, Illinois 60712
Ground Floor, 59 Gloucester Place, London W1U 8JJ
www.pilbooks.com
Permission is never granted for commercial purposes.
Manufactured in China.
ISBN 1-4127-3013-9

It was the start of a new day of school.

"Now, class," said Mrs. Hen, "today we will be learning how to add numbers."

As Mrs. Hen turned her back to the class and began to write on the chalkboard, Piggy got up from his desk.

"Whoops. I need to use the restroom," Piggy said. "Be right back, everybody!"

"Bye, Piggy!" said Bunny.

Before Piggy could dash out the door, Mrs. Hen turned around.

"Piggy," she said, "if you need to be excused, you must raise your hand and ask, 'May I be excused?'"

"I'm sorry," said Piggy. "May I be excused?"

"Yes you may," said Mrs. Hen, and Piggy quietly left the room. "Remember, class," she continued, "always ask to be excused."

Later that day, Mrs. Hen was helping the class do a neat science project.

"Zoom!" shouted Skunk.

"Yay!" yelled Puppy.

Mrs. Hen turned around to find the two friends playing with a paper airplane.

"Puppy and Skunk," she said, "this is science time. You will have time to play during recess."

"Please excuse us, Mrs. Hen," said Skunk. "We're sorry."

After the science project was finished, it was time for recess.

"Hooray!" said Hippo. "I love recess. It's my favorite!"

Piggy and Kitty also liked recess. They were in a hurry to get outside.

"Move it!" shouted Kitty.

"Get out of my way!" Piggy yelled. He gave Hippo a push.

"Aw, shucks," said Hippo. "All you had to do was say 'excuse me' and I would've moved."

After lunch, it was Hippo's turn to read in front of the class. He was already nervous enough, but then something terrible happened. Kitty burped! The class started laughing . . . everyone except Hippo.

"Oh, Kitty," said Mrs. Hen. "I know it was an accident, but what should you say?"

"Excuse me," said Kitty. "I'm sorry, Hippo."

"Children," Mrs. Hen said, "today you have not been using your manners. I think it's time for a quick review. What do you say if you need to leave class?"

"Excuse me," said Bear.

"And what if you interrupt someone?" asked Mrs. Hen.

"Excuse me," said Kitty.

"Good," said Mrs. Hen. "I want you all to remember your manners."

"Now, who wants to read for the class?" asked Mrs. Hen.

Bunny raised her hand and asked, "Excuse me. May I?"

But, at the same time, Mouse raised her hand and asked to read as well.

"Excuse me," said Mouse. "You asked first, Bunny. Please go ahead."

"Thank you," Bunny said. "That's very nice of you."

Mrs. Hen beamed with pride. Her class had learned to say "excuse me."

Excuse Me

As Mrs. Hen's class learned, when you are in class, at home, or with friends, it is important to say "excuse me" if you have to interrupt, you want to leave the room, you bump into someone, or if you burp.

When they reached the classroom, Skunk, who had been studying for a test, wanted to know all about Hippo's heroics. Hippo reenacted the moment.

"I stepped back, raced forward and then . . . boom!"

Hippo swung his leg forward and bumped into Mrs. Hen's desk, sending her favorite flower crashing to the floor.

Embarrassed, Hippo and the rest of his classmates sat quietly at their desks as Mrs. Hen walked in and saw her flower lying on the floor.

"She must be furious," thought Hippo. "It was an accident. I don't want to get in trouble."

So Hippo sat quietly all day, afraid to tell Mrs. Hen about his mistake.

At lunch Hippo could hardly eat.

"You should've told Mrs. Hen what happened," said Kitty.

"Yeah," Puppy agreed. "Now you've made things worse."

Hippo knew his friends were right, but he was too afraid of Mrs. Hen's reaction to do the right thing.

Piggy tried his best to cheer up his friend, but it was no use.

Hippo went back to the classroom early. He wanted to explain himself to Mrs. Hen, but he still couldn't tell the truth.

"Mrs. Hen," he said timidly, "I think I know what happened to your flowerpot. I saw a model airplane flying around. It could've flown in here and knocked your flower over."

Lying just made him feel worse.

That night Hippo had trouble falling asleep. He replayed the accident over and over in his mind.

"You've got to be honest," he thought. "That's the only way you're ever going to feel better about yourself."

Of course, after promising himself that he would tell the truth, Hippo fell fast asleep.

The next morning Hippo went to visit Mrs. Hen.

"I'm sorry," he said, "but I broke your flowerpot. I'm sorry I lied to you."

"It's okay," said Mrs. Hen. "I'm just glad you finally told the truth. Doesn't it feel better to be honest?"

"Yes, it does," said Hippo. "I feel better already."

Be Honest

Honesty means telling the truth, and it is always best to tell the truth... even when it isn't so easy to do. As Hippo learned, being honest always works out for the best.